Lucy's Lovey

Lucy's Lovey

Betsy Devany

illustrated by Christopher Denise

Christy Ottaviano Books
Henry Holt and Company
New York

Henry Holt and Company, LLC
Publishers since 1866
175 Fifth Avenue
New York, New York 10010
mackids.com

Library of Congress Cataloging-in-Publication Data
Names: Devany, Betsy, author. | Denise, Christopher, illustrator.
Title: Lucy's lovey / Betsy Devany ; illustrated by Christopher Denise.
Description: First edition. | New York : Henry Holt and Company, 2016. | Summary: Lucy had seventeen
doll babies but Smelly Baby was her favorite, so when the doll goes missing, Lucy is sad until it is
returned and eventually, after taking her with her everywhere, becomes smellier than ever.
Identifiers: LCCN 2015034858 | ISBN 9781627791472 (hardback)
Subjects: | CYAC: Dolls—Fiction. | Smell—Fiction. | BISAC: JUVENILE FICTION /
Toys, Dolls, Puppets. | JUVENILE FICTION / Social Issues / Friendship.
Classification: LCC PZ7.1.D486 Lu 2016 | DDC [E]—dc23
LC record available at https://lccn.loc.gov/2015034858

Our books may be purchased in bulk for promotional, educational, or business use.
Please contact your local bookseller or the Macmillan Corporate and Premium Sales Department at
(800) 221-7945 ext. 5442 or by e-mail at MacmillanSpecialMarkets@macmillan.com.

First Edition—2016 / Book designed by Patrick Collins
Printed in China by Toppan Leefung Printing Ltd., Dongguan City, Guangdong Province

1 3 5 7 9 10 8 6 4 2

For well-loved stuffies and dollies,
and the children who love them unconditionally
—B. D.

For Esmé
—C. D.

Lucy had seventeen doll babies.

Squeaky Baby,

Cry Baby,

Fancy Baby,

Tiny Baby.

Sparkly Baby,

Humongous Baby,

Flat Baby,   Burper Baby.

There were
babies called Doe,

Minky,

WaWa,

and Pinkie.

Baby Oopsie,

Filthy Franny,

Almost-Nakie,

and Bubba Bea.

But Lucy's favorite,
without question, was
Smelly Baby.

Grandma Nell had given the cloth doll to
Lucy, and when Lucy first kissed it, she said,
"She smells like peppermint."

Which is why Lucy named her Smelly Baby.

Smelly Baby went
everywhere with Lucy.

She ate with Lucy,

played with Lucy,

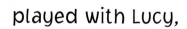

and only *she* slept in Lucy's bed.

With her own little smelly blanket, too.

Over time, Smelly Baby smelled less like peppermint and more like peanut butter. And bananas. And sour milk. With an occasional whiff of spaghetti.

Smelly Baby's arms began to pull away from her body, since Lucy would swing her in circles so the doll could dance in the breeze.

Smelly Baby didn't mind, because she knew she was Lucy's lovey.

One afternoon, Lucy's family visited Grandma Nell.

"Does that doll have to go everywhere?" said Lucy's sister, Ivy. "She stinks!"

"Does NOT!" Lucy breathed in her lovey's scent, then let Stasher take a sniff, too.

"Smelly Baby smells *perfect*. Right, Stasher?"

Stasher drooled in agreement. He *loved* stuffies. Especially noisy ones. He had more stinky, squeaky stuffies than Lucy had baby dolls. All of which were caked in Stasher drool.

Since Stasher's favorite game was sniff-and-swipe, Lucy had Smelly Baby nap in a cradle on top of Grandma Nell's bed.

Later, when it was time to go home, the doll
and the dog were nowhere in sight.

"Stasher!" Lucy yelled.

"Oh dear," said Grandma Nell,
who was used to Stasher
swiping stinky stuffies, and she
quickly showed Lucy all of
Stasher's secret stashes.
     None of which led to Smelly Baby.

"Did you check beneath the bed?" Ivy asked. "I bet Mr. Slobber's hiding there."

And sure enough, there was Stasher with Lucy's lovey.

"*Eew*," said Ivy. "I am *not* riding home with that dribbling doll mess of drool."

"Yes, you are," said Lucy.

To keep everyone happy, Grandma Nell slipped Smelly Baby into a bag.

"Tie it up," said Ivy. "Tight!"

"How will she breathe?" asked Lucy.

So Grandma Nell adjusted the bag beneath Smelly Baby's arms.

On the ride home, the car reeked. Even with most of Smelly Baby in the now smelly bag.

"Open the window," suggested Mom.

"Open *two*," begged Dad.

"And throw that doll out," added Ivy.

"Never," said Lucy, who held tight to Smelly Baby's arm.

"Be careful with your doll," warned Mom.

"I *am*," said Lucy.

But the faster the car went, the more Smelly Baby flapped like a flag in the breeze.

Whoopa whoopa whoopa went Smelly Baby, and then . . .

With that, the *whoopa whoopa whoopa* stopped, and all that remained of Lucy's lovey was . . .

Smelly Baby's smelly arm.

"SMELLY BABY!"

"Turn the car around!" said Ivy.

"Lovey on the loose!" Mom told Dad.

Quickly, Dad searched while Ivy and Mom comforted Lucy in the car. But when Dad returned with only his flashlight, Lucy knew.

"She's gone," Lucy finally said. "My Smelly Baby is *gone.*"

That night, it was hard for Lucy to sleep without her favorite doll.

So, one by one, Ivy brought Lucy her other babies. Squeaky Baby, Cry Baby, Fancy Baby, Tiny Baby. Sparkly Baby, Humongous Baby, Flat Baby, Burper Baby. Doe, Minky, WaWa, and Pinkie. Baby Oopsie, Filthy Franny, Almost-Nakie, Bubba Bea.

And Smelly Baby's smelly arm.

From then on, Lucy carried Smelly Baby's arm
everywhere.

"Does that stinky arm need to eat with us, too?"
asked Ivy.

"Yes," said Lucy. "It's all that's left of Smelly Baby,
and I . . . *really* miss her."

Both Ivy and Grandma Nell tried to help Lucy feel
better. Ivy gave Lucy one of her old dolls, while
Grandma Nell bought a new one.

Dolly Hand-Me-Down and Stasher Apology Baby joined
the other babies on the bed, where at night Lucy would
wish for Smelly Baby to somehow find her way home.

A few days later, a package arrived in the mail
for Lucy.

Dear Lucy,

I found your doll on the side of the road. How smart of you to write your name and address on her tummy! I could not find her missing arm, though I gave her a nice bath.

Sincerely,
Mrs. Fisher

Slowly, Lucy peeled back the tissue paper until her favorite doll looked up at her.

"My Smelly Baby!"

And then, as Lucy always did, she lifted the doll to her nose. She took a big sniff.

"You don't smell like you," Lucy said sadly.

"Thank goodness," Ivy said.

"But that's why I loved her the best."

"You are so weird," said Ivy.

Off the bed went the other baby dolls. On the bed went No Longer Smelly Baby.

"I miss old Smelly Baby," said Lucy.

No Longer Smelly Baby seemed to agree. So with her family's help, Lucy set out to fix her doll.

"Now you just need extra attention," Lucy said.

Which is exactly what Lucy gave Smelly
Baby. She dragged her through the
park, played with her in the sandbox,

and made sure her
doll was well fed.

Until, over time . . .

Smelly Baby was smellier than she'd ever been before. Which made at least Lucy very happy.

THE END